Roger Stevens lives in Brighton, where he can often be found sitting on the beach, gazing at the horizon, trying to think of a rhyme for seagull, ocean and pebble. He is the author of many children's books, including three solo collections of poems for Macmillan Children's Books, anthologies, novels and much more besides.

When not scribbling things into his notebook, he performs in a band and visits schools, festivals and libraries, performing his poems, making people laugh and encouraging everyone to read more poetry. Visit his award-winning website at www.poetryzone.co.uk

Roger is really happy to be working with Dyslexia Action.

Sarah Nayler was born in Southend-on-Sea. Severely dyslexic, she is delighted to be working on a project for a cause so close to her heart. She lives in Hertfordshire with her family and several accident-prone pets.

Poems chosen by Roger Stevens

Illustrated by Sarah Nayler

MACMILLAN CHILDREN'S BOOKS

For Joseph

First published 2009 by Macmillan Children's Books
a division of Macmillan Publishers Limited
20 New Wharf Road, London N1 9RR
Basingstoke and Oxford
Associated companies throughout the world
www.panmacmillan.com

ISBN 978-0-330-46865-7

3 5 7 9 8 6 4 2

A CIP catalogue record for this book is available from
the British Library.

Printed and bound in China

Contents

A Warning to Grown-Ups   viii

Nothing Else	Kit Wright	1
All About Poets	Trevor Parsons	2
The All-Purpose Children's Poem	Roger McGough	3
Words in Space	Michael Rosen	5
The Side Up Down Poem	Andrew Fusek Peters	6
Weightlessness	Roger Stevens	7
Rolling Down a Hill	Colin West	8
Metropoem	Celina Macdonald	9
Second Look at the Proverbs	Gerard Benson	9
The Colour of My Dreams	Peter Dixon	10
Nought to Nine	Rachel Rooney	12
Lost Proprty Ofice	John Rice	14
Hey Diddle Diddle	Roger Stevens	16
High Queue	Bernard Young	17
The Moon Speaks	James Carter	18
Snake	Catherine Benson	19
Sssss . . .	Gerard Benson	20
Elephant	Sue Hardy-Dawson	21
My Cousin Melda	Grace Nichols	22
Wonder Dogs for Sale	Violet Macdonald	23
Llama, Llama	Michaela Morgan	24
You Have Been Warned	Liz Brownlee	25

Mr and Mrs Peacock	Sue Hardy-Dawson	26
Crick Crack Crocodile	Joan Poulson	27
Rex	Jane Clarke	28
Hedgehog Hugs	Liz Brownlee	30
Neversaurus	Celia Warren	30
Canine Kenning	James Carter	31
Little Miss Muffet	Ian Bland	32
Suspense Haiku	Roger Stevens	32
The Grand Old Count of York	John Foster	33
A Wonderful Week	Julia Rawlinson	34
Monster Sale!!!	Clare Bevan	35
Mum's Umbrage	Graham Denton	35
Medusa's Bad-Hair Days	Brian Moses	36
Laughter	John Agard	38
There's a Lot I've Not Seen	Nick Toczek	39
Fed Up?	Michaela Morgan	40
Grandpa's Soup	Jackie Kay	42
No Longer My Hero	Philip Waddell	44
Biscuit Poem	Tony Mitton	44
For the Soup	John Hegley	45
Mum Says . . .	Judith Nicholls	46
Fruit Jokes	Adrian Mitchell	47
Never Trust a Lemon	Roger Stevens	48
Here Lies Mad Lil	Jan Dean	49
Beware! Take Care!	Ian Billings	50
Pupil Troubles	Graham Denton	51
Whizz Kid	Gina Douthwaite	52

Short Visit, Long Stay	Paul Cookson	53
The Triangular Cruise	Andrea Shavick	54
The Magician	Michael Leigh	55
A Sight for Sore Eyes	Robert Scotellaro	56
Grandad on My Scooter	Justin Coe	57
Making a Meal of It	Bernard Young	58
The Winning Goal	Roger Stevens	59
My Mum Put Me on the Transfer List	David Harmer	60
We've Got a Girl in Our Team	John Coldwell	61
Little Lee	Jill Townsend	62
Victoria's Poem	Fred Sedgwick	63
Unfair	Rachel Rooney	64
Actions Speak	Paul Cookson	66
The Roman Baths	Chrissie Gittins	67
Smile Please	Eric Finney	68
Valentine from a Scientist	Celina Macdonald	69
When We Grow Up	Steven Herrick	70
Science Lesson	Mike Johnson	72
Choosing a Book	Celia Warren	73
Not Stupid	Daphne Kitching	74
The Jumble Boy	Justin Coe	76
Bedtime Mysteries	Philip Waddell	78
Afterword		81
About Dyslexia Action		82
Acknowledgements		84

A Warning to Grown-Ups

Poetry is fun. Do not spoil it.

Do not make children read this book for homework. If you do you may be vaporized by a death ray.

Poems are allowed to have rude words because they are literature, so bum to you.

Do not ask children how these poems make them feel. It is a stupid question.

Do not try to analyse these poems: they may self-detonate.

If you can't see the sense of it, that's probably your fault.

Poems do not have to be written in grammatical sentences or have correct punctuation, so nurch.

Do not tell people off for daydreaming.
Poems come from daydreams.

Never make anyone copy out a poem. It
spoils it.

Do not make children read these poems
aloud in front of the whole class. If you do,
you will be kidnapped by aliens and taken to
Alpha Centauri and forced to mark Year Six
homework for a thousand years.

*Issued by the Galactic Authority and dictated
by telepathy to* **Ken Follett***, who wrote it all
down with no crossings out*

Nothing Else

There's nothing I can't see
From here
There's nothing I can't be
From here

Because my eyes
Are open wide
To let the big
World come inside

I think I can see me
From here

Kit Wright

All About Poets

A poet is for life
not just for Christmas Day.
Stroking a silky-haired poet
can soothe your troubles away.
A long-haired breed of poet
should always be kept well-groomed.
Keep their sleeping-quarters
in a draught-free part of the room.
Do not indulge your poet
with titbits from your plate.
Encourage regular exercise
to avoid excessive weight.
It is generally thought unhealthy
to have poets in your bed.
Be sensitive about disposal
once your poet is dead.
Sorry, I meant to say 'pet'.

Trevor Parsons

The All-Purpose Children's Poem

The first verse contains a princess
Two witches (one evil, one good)
There is a castle in it somewhere
And a dark and tangled wood.

The second has ghosts and vampires
Monsters with foul-smelling breath
It sends shivers down the book spine
And scares everybody to death.

The third is one of my favourites
With rabbits in skirts and trousers
Who talk to each other like we do
And live in neat little houses.

The fourth verse is bang up to date
And in it anything goes
Set in the city, it doesn't rhyme
(Although, in a way it does).

The fifth is set in the future
(And as you can see, it's the last)
When the Word was made Computer
And books are a thing of the past.

Roger McGough

Words in Space

They decided to abolish the words:
to sit
to stand
and to lie
and the word
to float will replace them.

So people now say:
float up straight when I'm talking to you
let sleeping dogs float
let's float down and have a chat about it.

People who don't like cabbage say:
I can't float cabbage
and they watch telly
in the floating room.

Is there anyone who doesn't
underfloat what I'm saying?

Michael Rosen

The Side Up Down Poem

Wash your ears, Mum said.
So I took them off
And stuck them in the washing machine.
Clean your room, Dad said.
So I rolled it up
And shook it out of the window.
Make the breakfast, my brother said.
So I did –
With bits of balsa wood and modelling glue.
Feed the cat, my auntie said.
So I fed him . . .
To the dog!
Take your time, Dad said.
So I packed up the clocks
And I flew to Mars
Where the days fly by
Wearing nothing but stars.

Andrew Fusek Peters

Burp

Weightlessness

As the spaceship turns into the planet's pull
Weightlessness

As the teacher looks up from her book
And sees you just about
To throw the paper dart
Weightlessness

As the sandman drapes
The cape of darkness
On your half-formed thoughts
Weightlessness

Before you are born, when you are gone
Weightlessness

Roger Stevens

Rolling Down a Hill

I'm rolling
rolling
rolling
down

I'm rolling
down a
hill.

I'm rolling
rolling
down

I'm rolling
down it still.

I'm rolling
rolling
rolling
down

I'm rolling
down a
hill.

I'm rolling
rolling
rolling
down

But now
I'm feeling
ill.

Colin West

Metropoem

I am wri ting this po em
Tick tick tick tick tick tick tick
To a met ro nome
Tick tick tick tick tick
So if I get just one beat wrong
Tick tick tick tick tick tick tick tick
It' ll hit me with a ve ry long
Stick tick tick tick tick tick tick tick tick.

Celina Macdonald

Second Look at the Proverbs

People who live in glass-houses
Should watch it while changing their trouziz

Gerard Benson

The Colour of My Dreams

I am a really rotten reader
the worst in all the class
the sort of rotten reader
that makes you want to laugh.

I'm last in all the readin' tests
my score's not on the page
and when I read to teacher
she gets in such a rage.

She says I cannot form my words
she says I can't build up
and that I don't know phonics
– and don't know c-a-t from k-u-p.

They say that I'm dyslexic
(that's a word they've just found out)
. . . but when I get some plasticine
I know what that's about.

I make these scary monsters
I draw these secret lands
and get my hair all sticky
and paint on all me hands.

I make these super models
I build these smashing towers
that reach up to the ceiling
and take me hours and hours.

I paint these lovely pictures
in thick green drippy paint
that gets all on the carpet
and makes the cleaners faint.

I build great magic forests
weave bushes out of string
and paint pink panderellos
and birds that really sing.

I play my world of real believe
I play it every day
and people stand and watch me
but don't know what to say.

They give me diagnostic tests
they try out reading schemes
but none of them will ever know
the colour of my dreams.

Peter Dixon

Nought to Nine

A ring made of gold, a doughnut and hole,
something that's nothing that's easy to roll.

A periscope raised, a walking stick,
the cut of a cake and a candle's new wick.

A swan on a lake, a nun knelt in prayer,
an FA Cup handle raised in the air.

The pout of a mouth, a bird flying over,
a bra on a line, two leaves of a clover.

A neatly pressed ribbon, a kite without string,
the nose of a witch and an arm in a sling.

The hand of a pirate, a flat-headed snake,
an apple divided, the latch on a gate.

A teardrop to wipe, a cherry and stalk,
the speech mark to use when your words start
   to talk.

Half a triangle, a fox's ear-tip,
an arrow, an arm of a hand on a hip.

Balancing balls and a circular kiss,
a hoop with a waist and a rope in a twist.

A hook in a curtain, chameleon's tongue,
the whistle to blow when this poem is done.

Rachel Rooney

Lost Proprty Ofice

Pair of sunglases.
A walking stic.
Flowr pot.
A trumpt.
A child's tedy bear.
Gentlman's brown hat.
Nike runing shoe (left foot).
Box of white candls.
A libray book.
Pilow case (with embroidered elephant).
Set of fals teeth.
Plastic bnana.
Tenis racket.
Hot-water bttle.
Pair of scisors.
Umbrela.
A child's Disny watch.
A mouse (not a real one – a cmputer mouse!)
Smal suitcase.

Green flask with red beakr.
Map of London undergrond.
Silver whisle.
Larg jar of Vaseline.
Nine e's
three l's
two n's
two o's
two s's
one a
one d
one f
one k
one r
one t
and one u.
If lost, please find.

John Rice

Hey Diddle Diddle

Hey diddle diddle
The cat and the fiddle
The cow jumped over the bed
The little dog laughed
But not for long
Cos the cow landed right on his head

Roger Stevens

High Queue

On the mountain top
tourists politely queue to
photograph the view.

Bernard Young

The Moon Speaks

I, the moon,
would like it known - I
never **f**ollow people home. I
simply do not have the time. And
neither do I ever shine. For what you
often see at night is me reflecting solar
light. And I'm not cheese! No, none of
these: no mozzarellas, cheddars, bries, all
you'll find here if you please – are my
dusty, empty seas. And cows do not
jump over me. Now that is simply
lunacy! **Yo**u used to come and
visit me. Oh, do return,
I'm *lonely*, see.

James Carter

Snake

The sand is hot
my belly zip-zips over it,
drawing neat curves
that the wind rubs out.
I divine water
with my forked-twig tongue,
water held in the flesh
and blood of a desert rat.
With my polished skin
my lithe body
my sinuous movement
my unhingeing jaw
my engulfing maw
I surround my meal –
a long, long gulp,
a week's digestion.

Catherine Benson

Sssss . . .

Sly slitherer,
sloomy sidler;
slack slumberer,
doom dreamer.
Sleeve.
Tongue flickerer,
fanged hypnotist;
lazy looper,
knot tier.
Eve
whisperer.
Narrow fellow,
subtle beast,
limbless
poisoner.
Labyrinth.
Patterned
whiplash
in the grass.
Secret watcher.
Needle tooth,
cold eye,
letter S . . .
ssss
sss
ss
s

Gerard Benson

Elephant

The
elephant
is
often
blue,
for sadly
he will tend to
brood on all
the carnage
that he
caused, just
by walking back and
forth. His memory
for which he's famed
fills him with appalling
shame   for all   whose
end he   brought   to close
and   swiftly   vacuumed
with   his   nose.

Sue Hardy-Dawson

My Cousin Melda

My Cousin Melda
She don't make fun
She ain't afraid of anyone
Even mosquitoes
When they bite her
She does bite them back
And say –
'Now tell me, how you like that?'

Grace Nichols

Wonder Dogs for Sale

My dog can't fly or run or skip,
Or drag to air a sinking ship,
He can't fly planes or sail a sub,
Or make things with a yogurt tub,
He cannot talk or shake your hand,
He can't jump like a rubber band,
My dog can't drive or navigate,
Or on a stick balance a plate,
He can't even go for a walk,
Let alone draw with a chalk,
They said he could when I bought him,
'Wonder dogs, so fit and trim!'
And now the streets are cleared of fog,
I'm not too sure it is a dog.

Violet Macdonald

Llama, Llama

A llama, a llama
will keep your sheep calmer
yes that's what a llama will do.
It's not just a charmer
it can be an alarmer
and see off a hungry bear too.
There's no need of armour
if you keep a llama
it's more than a big snooty sheep.
So go get your pyjamas
you weary old farmers
at last you can stop counting sheep.
Yes a llama, a llama's
a friend to the farmer
a friend to the chicken and sheep.
No panic and drama
if you have a llama –
just sweet dreams, quiet fields . . .
    and deep sleep.

Michaela Morgan

You Have Been Warned

Hippo bottoms have such expanse,
they can't afford the cost of pants,
so should one turn up miniskirted,
be sure to keep your eyes averted . . .

Liz Brownlee

Mr and Mrs Peacock

It is
    really
        most
            ex
            tr
            ao
            rd
            in
            ar
            y
                how
            much the
            pea he and
            she vary. He
        seems so regal
        and uncaring,
        loudly proudly
            overbearing.
                Always magnificently
                    attired, with a tail that is
                        inspired. A hundred eyes
                            gold, green and purple, trailed or
                            fanned out in a circle. His wife she
                            wears a quieter gown, but feels
                            it's he who lets them down.
                                He may have beauty,
                                grace and poise,
                                    but makes a
                                    truly rotten
                                    noise.

Sue Hardy-Dawson

Crick Crack Crocodile
(For George)

Crick, crack, crocodile,
what bright shiny teeth,
what a fierce, dark smile.

I wouldn't like to meet you
when you're hungry or sad.
I'd shout: Mr Crocodile,
I taste very bad.

But I'd be glad to see you
in your jungle, by the river –
strong tail, scaly back,
handsome water dragon.

Crick, crack, crick, crack, Snap!

Joan Poulson

Rex

'Come on in, don't mind Rex,
he's very tame, you'll see.
Sit down. Oh look! Rex likes you,
his head is on your knee.

Yes, I've worked hard to train him
since he hatched out of his egg.
Rex can fetch, and walk to heel,
roll over, sit and beg.

He loves his tummy tickled,
he never goes out straying.
Well, yes, he bit my arm off,
but he was only playing.

He's licking you? He licks me too!
Don't worry, Rex adores us.
You want to know what breed he is?
He's a Tyrannosaurus.

Don't run away! He'll think you're prey.
He can smell your fear.
Bad boy, Rex! That's playing rough.
Down, Rex! Down!

Oh dear . . .'

Jane Clarke

Hedgehog Hugs

A hedgehog's hug is mainly hid
beneath its sharp and spiky lid,
and when it rolls into a ball
a hedgehog has no hug at all!

Liz Brownlee

Neversaurus

When dinosaurs roamed the earth,
So huge, it was easy to spot 'em,
You'd frequently see a triceratops
But never a tricerabottom.

Celia Warren

Canine Kenning
or Ha – Wooooooo Am I?

Furry – fella
forest – dweller

toothy – terror
tame me? – never!

lunar – lover
piggy – puffer

chimney – dropper
come – a – cropper

Hoody – charmer
Granny – harmer

hunter – hater
terminator

wisest – creature
want – to – eat – ya!

Beastly? Yes!
But I'm the best!
The Big Bad Wolf . . .
had you guessed?

James Carter

Little Miss Muffet

Little Miss Muffet
Sat on a tuffet
Eating a strawberry pavlova
Along came a spider and
Sat down beside her
And ate the bits she had left over!

Ian Bland

Suspense Haiku

It's unexpected.
Midnight. A knock on the door.
You open it. Oh . . .

Roger Stevens

The Grand Old Count of York

The Grand Old Count of York
He had ten thousand bats.
He kept them in his wardrobe
Hanging from his cloaks and hats.
And when he went out they flew out.
And when he went in they flew in.
And when they were neither in nor out
They haunted his neighbours' flats.

John Foster

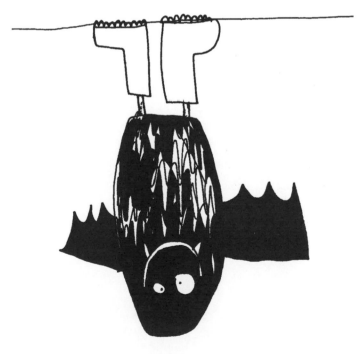

A Wonderful Week

On Monday I'm sure I heard a dragon,
Giving a mighty roar.
Teacher said it was just the pipes,
Rumbling under the floor.
On Tuesday I'm sure I saw a witch,
Swooping across the sky.
Teacher said it was just a scrap
Of dark cloud drifting by.
On Wednesday I'm sure I whiffed a wizard,
Cooking up a spell.
Teacher said it was just the lunchtime
Stew that I could smell.
On Thursday I'm sure I saw a ghost,
Up on the bell-tower roof.
Teacher said it was just a pigeon,
Fluttering home to roost.
On Friday I sat and thought for a bit.
Teacher is probably right.
But school isn't going to be half such fun,
With nothing to give me a fright.

Julia Rawlinson

Monster Sale!!!

MONSTER SALE!!! the advert said,
I'm telling you – it LIED.
There was junk galore
In the superstore . . .
But not ONE monster inside.

Clare Bevan

Mum's Umbrage

The teacher called my mother
on my first day back at school –
he told her I'd been naughty
and behaving like a fool.
'Now just you wait a minute,'
came my mother's quick response,
'he misbehaved all summer
and I never called *you* once!'

Graham Denton

Medusa's Bad-Hair Days

Although she's tried
every kind of shampoo
nothing works
on Medusa's hairdo.

Her snakes are always
in a tangle,
coiling and spitting
at every angle.

They won't keep quiet,
they won't stay still,
these bickering serpents
are making her ill.

She needs a hero
to hack at her hair,
someone the flickering tongues
won't scare.

A hero willing
to take a chance,
to cut and to kill
without meeting her glance.

A blindfolded hero
acting alone,
someone whose bones
won't turn to stone.

And she's vowed that
    she'll change
her reptilian ways
if someone can rid her
of bad-hair days.

She'll change from the woman
you love to hate,
if someone would ask her
out on a date.

(Are you brave enough
to fall in love
with Medusa?)

Brian Moses

Laughter

Laughter can be hairy
Laughter can be smooth
Laughter can be polite
Laughter can be rude

Laughter can catch you by day
Laughter can catch you by night
And don't you ever forget
Laughter can make you wet

yourself.

John Agard

There's a Lot I've Not Seen

I've seen no sunbathers at night.
I've seen no pens taught how to write.
I've seen no combs with teeth that bite.
I've seen no chair-legs learn to walk.
I've seen no knife that kissed a fork.
I've seen no pig dine out on pork.
I've seen no thirty-foot-tall elves.
I've seen no books climb on their shelves.
I've seen no meals consume themselves.
I've seen no puddle waterproof.
I've seen no sea horse stamp its hoof.
I've seen no cellar on a roof.
I've seen no tree that won a race.
I've seen no shoe tie its own lace.
I've seen no fish in outer space.
I've seen no sky that's been bright green.
I've seen no jack that beats a queen.
I've seen no twelve that's called twoteen . . .
I've seen no things that I've not seen.

Nick Toczek

Fed Up?

Stuff your belly
Fill your face
Pack a snack
Leave no space
Scoff the lot
Shovel it up
Throw it down
(Don't throw it up)
Ram it, jam it
Choke and chew it.
Wolf it down
You can do it!
Nibble it, nosh it
Squeeze and squash it.
Munch and crunch it, gulp and slurp
(Pausing only for a burp).

A bit of sauce – just a squirt
You did save room for dessert?
Another nibble? A bone to chew?
Speak up clearly. I can't HEAR you.
There's lots of food
No need to stop
What's that you're saying?
Oh . . . look out . . . POP!
Now that IS messy
That is RUDE!
I think that you had
TOO MUCH FOOD.

Michaela Morgan

Grandpa's Soup

No one makes soup like my Grandpa's,
with its diced carrots the perfect size
and its diced potatoes the perfect size
and its wee soft bits –
what are their names? –
and its big bit of hough,
which rhymes with loch, floating
like a rich island in the middle of the soup sea.

I say, Grandpa, Grandpa, your soup is the
    best soup in the whole world.
And Grandpa says, Och,
which rhymes with hough and loch,
Och, don't be daft,
because he's shy about his soup, my
    Grandpa.
He knows I will grow up and pine for it.
I will fall ill and desperately need it.
I will long for it my whole life after he is gone.
Every soup will become sad and wrong after
    he is gone.

He knows when I'm older I will avoid soup
  altogether.
Oh Grandpa, Grandpa, why is your soup so
  glorious? I say,
tucking into my fourth bowl in a day.

Barley! That's the name of the wee soft bits.
  Barley.

Jackie Kay

No Longer My Hero

I thought my dad was
Batman . . . but he only plays
cricket for England.

Philip Waddell

Biscuit Poem

Why
does the first biscuit
in each new pack,
when I try
to prise it out,
have to . . .

wait for it . . .

CRACK!?

Tony Mitton

For the Soup

There once was an organic leek
That had managed to learn how to speak.
At the sight of a knife
It would fear for its life
And go eeeeeeeeeeeeeeeeeeeeeeeeeeeeeee
  eeeeeeeeeeek!

John Hegley

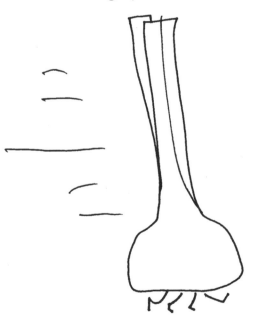

Mum Says . . .

Eat up your apple,
eat your ice cream,
eat up your jelly,
your strawberry-dream!
Eat up your biscuits
and chocolate cake,
your trifle and cream
for goodness sake
or you'll get

NO

CABBAGE!

Judith Nicholls

Fruit Jokes

The satsuma
Has no sense of humour
But a fig'll
Giggle

Adrian Mitchell

Never Trust a Lemon

Never trust a lemon
It's a melon in disguise
Never trust potatoes
With shifty eyes
Never trust a radish
It repeats all that it hears
Never trust an onion
It will all end in tears

Roger Stevens

Here Lies Mad Lil

Here lies Mad Lil the dinner lady
In this spot that's cool and shady.
She used to be all rant and rave-y
Now she's buried in her grave-y.

Jan Dean

Beware! Take Care!

Our school caretaker, Mr Mole,
Didn't take care – so he fell in a hole.
When your job is about taking care,
If there's a hole in the ground you should
    beware.

Ian Billings

(PS – Don't worry about the hole in the ground
– the police are looking into it.)

Pupil Troubles

There once was a teacher, Miss Wright,
Whose lessons affected her sight.
Through all of her classes
She sported dark glasses –
Her students were simply too bright!

Graham Denton

Whizz Kid

Beth's the best at reading,
Gary's good at sums,
Kirsty's quick at counting
on her fingers and her thumbs,
Wayne's all right at writing,
Charles has lots of chums,
but I'm the fastest out of school
when home time comes.

Gina Douthwaite

Short Visit, Long Stay

The school trip was a special occasion
But we never reached our destination
Instead of the zoo
I was locked in the loo
Of an M62 service station.

Paul Cookson

The Triangular Cruise

We went for a cruise round Bermuda
The Captain got ruder and ruder
He threw us into the sea and
forgot us. But in case
you're wondering
what got us, it
wasn't the
Triangle,
it was
the
barracuda!

Andrea Shavick

The Magician

The magician with wry grimaces
Finds things in most unusual places

He reaches round behind my ear
And finds a hamster hiding there

From nowhere comes a singing bird
And then he says the magic word

From his empty hat there jumps a rabbit.
It's escaping.

Someone grab it!

Too late . . .

Michael Leigh

A Sight for Sore Eyes

A wacky optometrist, Delf,
Took some eye lenses off of the shelf
AND JUST TO BE HORRID
Glued twelve to his forehead
Made a spectacle out of himself

Robert Scotellaro

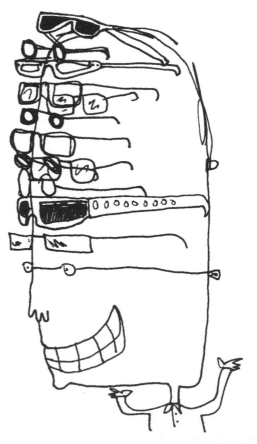

Grandad on My Scooter

Grandad's still a bad lad
A Trojan and a trooper
And no man can move faster than
Grandad on my scooter

Woe betide you if he's behind you
And you don't hear his hooter
Pension power, ninety miles an hour
It's Grandad on my scooter

He never breaks, just overtakes
And always gets there sooner
A rare daredevil, freewheeling rebel
Grandad on my scooter

Straight from the past, so super fast
He's flying to the future
Where it's all downhill, chased by the Bill
It's Grandad on my scooter

Justin Coe

Making a Meal of It

What did you do at school today?
Played football.
Where are you going now?
To play football.
What time will you be back?
After football.
Football! Football! Football!
That's all I ever hear.
Well?
Well don't be late for tea.
OK.
We're having football casserole.
Eh?
Followed by football crumble.
What?
Washed down with a . . .
As if I can't guess!
nice pot of . . .
I'm not listening!
tea.

Bernard Young

The Winning Goal

When I scored the winning goal
I had never felt so alone.
The crowd went crazy, on their feet
But my heart sank like a stone.
They say that scoring is marvellous,
The best feeling that's ever been known.
But it's hard to take
When you make a mistake
And the back of the net
Is your own.

Roger Stevens

My Mum Put Me on the Transfer List

On offer:
one nippy striker, ten years old
has scored seven goals this season
has nifty footwork and a big smile
knows how to dive in the penalty box
can get filthy and muddy within two minutes
guaranteed to wreck his kit each week.
This is a FREE TRANSFER
but he comes with running expenses
weeks of washing shirts and shorts
socks and vests, a pair of trainers
needs to scoff huge amounts
of chips and burgers, beans and apples
pop and cola, crisps and oranges
endless packets of chewing gum.
This offer open until the end of the season
I'll have him back then
at least until the cricket starts.
Any takers?

David Harmer

We've Got a Girl in Our Team

We've got a girl in our team and it's against
　　the rules.
Girls were made for skipping not booting
　　footballs.
We've got a girl in our team and that's not
　　fair.
She won't want to head the ball and mess up
　　her hair.
We've got a girl in our team and it makes me
　　sick.
I suppose she'll do her make-up before each
　　free kick.
We've got a girl in our team and look what
　　she's done.
Scored in the last minute and our team's won.

John Coldwell

Little Lee

Thin Tim
and Tall Paul
playing footy
against a wall.
Little Lee
wants to play.
'Let me join in.'
'No,' they say.
Lee is quicker
than Tim or Paul –
he runs away
and takes their ball.

Jill Townsend

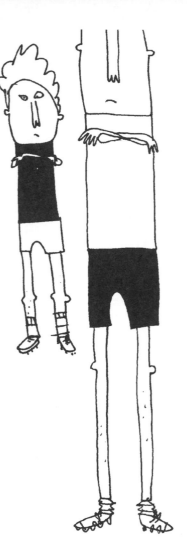

Victoria's Poem

Send me upstairs without any tea,
refuse me a plaster to stick on my knee.

Make me kiss Grandpa, who smells of his pipe,
make me eat beetroot, make me eat tripe.

Throw all my best dolls into the river,
make me eat bacon and onions – with liver.

Tell Mr Allan I've been a bad girl,
rename me Nellie, rename me Pearl.

But don't, even if
the world suddenly ends,
                    ever again, Mother,

wipe my face with a tissue
in front of my friends.

Fred Sedgwick

Unfair

She picked the fight
but now she cries.
I know I'm right.
She's telling lies

but now she cries
for sympathy.
She's telling lies
and Dad blames me.

For sympathy
she dabs her face
and Dad blames me.
I'm in disgrace.

She dabs her face,
she gets a hug.
I'm in disgrace,
she's looking smug.

She gets a hug,
I want to cry.
She's looking smug
I'm sure that's why

I want to cry.
I know I'm right.
I'm sure that's why
she picked the fight.

Rachel Rooney

Actions Speak

He never said a word, my brother.
Just brought me a tissue – or two –
a cup of tea, chocolate biscuits
and his copy of the *Beano*.

Left them on my bedside table,
squeezed my shoulder, smiled
and left me alone for a while.

Never said a word.
Never had to.
Knew just how I felt.

Paul Cookson

The Roman Baths

I threw a coin into the sacred pool
And made a secret wish.

If I tell the wish
Then I will never have a friend,

If I tell the wish
Then wars will never end,

If I tell the wish
My angelfish might die,

If I tell the wish
I will always wonder why

I threw a stone in the sacred pool
And made a secret wish.

Chrissie Gittins

Smile Please

You're not very happy today,
You're not jolly, not joyful, not sunny.
I'd like to say something to cheer you up
But I can't think of anything funny.
On your face there's no trace of your usual
    smile –
It's nicer by far when you wear one.
Look here, if you can't find a smile for yourself,
Do have one of mine, I've a spare one.

Eric Finney

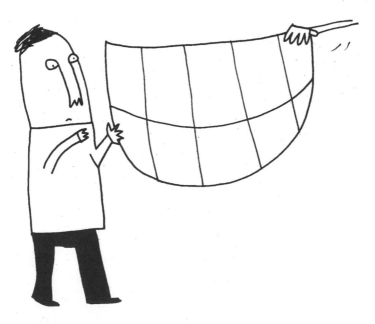

Valentine from a Scientist

It's not in your heart but in your head
That stops you from acting inane.
It's in the head that you feel fear
Or love or hate or pain.
The heart has naught to do with emotions,
It merely pumps blood through your veins.
So it might not sound that romantic but:
I love you with all my brain.

Celina Macdonald

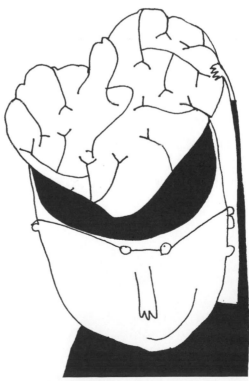

When We Grow Up

I thought it was a simple question really.
Ms Arthur asked each of us to stand up, in
    turn,
and say what we want to be
when we grow up.
The first five students said
Teacher
then Alastair said
Pilot
and we went slowly around the class
Builder
Doctor
Truck driver
Writer
Vet
Architect
Soldier
and when it was my turn
I stood up
and in a very clear voice, said,
a Dad.

Everyone giggled
as if I'd said something rude,
or silly.
The bell rang for recess
and I sat down again,
red-faced and confused.
It was the truth.
I wanted to be a Dad.
I've never seen my dad
and I wouldn't wish that
on anyone.

Steven Herrick

Science Lesson

We've done 'water' and 'metals' and
    'plastic',
Today it's the turn of 'elastic':
Teacher sets up a test;
Wow, that was the best –
He whizzed through the window. Fantastic!

Mike Johnson

Choosing a Book

When I'm in a book shop
They give me funny looks.
While others choose by title
Or blurb about the books;
By author's style, the cover
Or a name that rings a bell,
I sniff the books and choose one
By its quality of smell.

Celia Warren

Not Stupid

I'm eight
And I don't think I'm stupid,
But some things I can't understand.
Why, when I know that I'm trying so hard,
Does my pencil seem drunk in my hand?

I'm eight
And I don't think I'm stupid,
But reading just fills me with dread.
Why do the letters and words move around,
And their sounds get mixed up in my head?

I'm eight
And I don't think I'm stupid,
But spelling's confusing my brain.
Which clever person made rough rhyme with
     stuff?
And are those drops rein, reign or rain?

I'm eight
And I don't think I'm stupid,
But it hurts when I'm told I don't try.
I want to read and to write and to spell,
I want to so much, I could cry.

And sometimes I do.

Daphne Kitching

The Jumble Boy

He reads the same simple sentence again
The sense of it simply will not sink in
He's the Jumble Boy who can't spell his name

The panic runs manic about his brain
Letters give him jitters: jest and jinx him
He reads the same simple sentence again

But it's too hard for him. He can't explain
The problem is he can't stop from thinking
He's the Jumble Boy who can't spell his name

Teachers can't reach him but to shout his
    shame
He's not got a clue, they've not an inkling
He reads the same simple sentence again

One dreamday he'll teach them. He'll find his
    aim
And write the world such a verse worth
    printing
Of the Jumble Boy who can't spell his name

But now Jane likes Peter. Peter likes Jane
And he hates the school and all who shrink
   him
He reads the same simple sentence again
Just the Jumble Boy who can't spell his name

Justin Coe

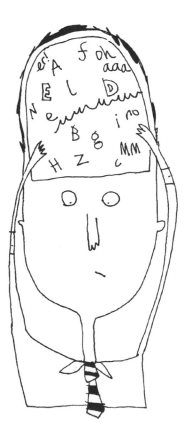

Bedtime Mysteries

Does Little Red Riding Hood
Rescue her gran?
Is the Pied Piper
A kindly young man?
Do Hansel and Gretel
Escape from the witch?
Do Jack's magic beans
Make the simple lad rich?
Is Goldilocks eaten up
By the three bears?
Are tortoises better
At racing than hares?
Is the old woman
In Snow White a fake?
Don't ask me, I don't know,
I can't stay awake!

Philip Waddell

Afterword

When I learned that many dyslexic children find it easier to read words written on yellow paper, I thought: Wouldn't a book of poems written on yellow paper look cool? I put the idea to the Dyslexia Action charity and the guys there liked it. Gaby Morgan, at Macmillan Children's Books, immediately understood my concern that many dyslexic children are denied access to the wealth of children's literature available today. A book they could actually read might go some way to redressing the balance. I approached several poets and they all agreed to donate poems and were very enthusiastic, as was Sarah Nayler, the illustrator, who is herself dyslexic. Justin Coe gave me 'The Jumble Boy' poem from his Jumble Book show, which is based on his experiences as a dyslexic youngster. He has lent me the title for this book, but I've promised to give it back one day. The poems in this collection are not just for dyslexic children, of course. They are for everybody. And the great thing is that by buying the book and enjoying the poems you will be contributing to the work of Dyslexia Action – a great cause.

Roger Stevens

PS I'd like to thank Linda Telfer.

Dyslexia is a hidden disability that predominately affects literacy development but also causes difficulties with mathematics, memory, organization and sequencing. The difficulties caused can seriously undermine confidence and self-esteem. Dyslexia is biological in origin and is seen to run in families, affecting up to ten per cent of the UK population to varying degrees. It does not affect intelligence and can affect anyone of any age and background.

Dyslexia should not be a barrier to success and there are some very brilliant and talented people across all professions who are dyslexic. However, for those whose difficulties are not recognized and addressed, it is too often the case that they underachieve, which comes not only at a huge cost to the individual but is also a waste of potential.

Dyslexia Action is a national charity and the UK's leading provider of services and support for people with dyslexia and literacy difficulties. We are committed to improving public policy and practice.

We partner with schools, local authorities, colleges, universities, employers, voluntary-sector organizations and Government to improve the quality and quantity of help for people with dyslexia and specific learning difficulties.

It is through generosity such as the royalties from this superb poetry book that we are able to help and support those we would otherwise not have been able to reach. On behalf of the individuals we help and support we thank everyone involved in *The Jumble Book*. With special thanks to Roger Stevens, Sarah Nayler and Ken Follett.

Dyslexia Action
Park House, Wick Road, Egham,
Surrey TW20 0HH
T 01784 222300
F 01784 222333
E info@dyslexiaaction.org.uk
W www.dyslexiaaction.org.uk
Registered charity No. 268502
Scottish registered charity No. SCO39177
Dyslexia Action is the working name for Dyslexia Institute Limited

Acknowledgements

The publishers wish to thank the following for permission to use copyright material:

John Agard, 'Laughter', by permission of the author; **Catherine Benson**, 'Snake', by permission of the author; **Gerard Benson**, 'Second Look at the Proverbs', first published in *How to Be Well-versed in Poetry*, ed. E. O. Parrott, Viking 1990, and 'Sssss . . .', both by permission of the author; **Clare Bevan**, 'Monster Sale!!!', first published in *Monster Poems*, ed. Brian Moses, Macmillan Children's Books 2005, by permission of the author; **Ian Billings**, 'Beware! Take Care!', by permission of the author; **Ian Bland**, 'Little Miss Muffet', by permission of the author; **Liz Brownlee**, 'You Have Been Warned' and 'Hedgehog Hugs', by permission of the author; **James Carter**, 'The Moon Speaks' and 'Canine Kenning', by permission of the author; **Jane Clarke,** 'Rex', by permission of the author; **Justin Coe**, 'Grandad on My Scooter' and 'The Jumble Boy', by permission of the author; **John Coldwell**, 'We've Got a Girl in Our Team' by permission of the author; **Paul Cookson**, 'Short Visit, Long Stay' and 'Actions Speak', by permission of the author; **Jan Dean**, 'Here Lies Mad Lil', by permission of the author; **Graham Denton**, 'Mum's Umbrage' and 'Pupil Troubles', by permission of the author; **Peter Dixon**, 'The Colour of My Dreams', first published in *The Colour of My Dreams*, Macmillan Children's Books 2002, by permission of the author; **Gina Douthwaite**, 'Whizz Kid', first published in *Countdown* by Ginn, by permission of the author; **Eric Finney**, 'Smile Please', by permission of the author; **John Foster**, 'The Grand Old Count of York', by permission of the author; **Andrew Fusek Peters**, 'The Side Up Down Poem', by permission of the author; **Chrissie Gittins**, 'The Roman Baths', first published in *Now You See Me, Now You . . .*, Rabbit Hole Publications 2002, by permission of the author; **Sue Hardy-Dawson**, 'Elephant' and 'Mr and Mrs Peacock', by permission of the author; **David Harmer**, 'My Mum Put Me on the Transfer List', by permission of the author; **John Hegley**, 'For the Soup', by permission of the author; **Steven Herrick**, 'When We Grow Up', by permission of the author; **Mike Johnson**, 'Science Lesson', by permission of the author; **Jackie Kay**, 'Grandpa's Soup', by permission of the author; **Daphne Kitching**, 'Not Stupid', first published in *As Long as There Are Trees*, Kingston Press 2001, by permission of the author; **Michael Leigh**, 'The Magician', by permission of the author; **Celina Macdonald**, 'Metropoem'and 'Valentine from a Scientist', by permission of the author; **Violet Macdonald**, 'Wonder Dogs for Sale', by permission of the author; **Roger McGough**, 'The All-Purpose Children's Poem', by permission of the author; **Adrian Mitchell**, 'Fruit Jokes', by permission of the author; **Tony Mitton**, 'Biscuit Poem', by permission of the author; **Michaela Morgan**, 'Llama, Llama' and 'Fed Up?', by permission of the author; **Brian Moses**, 'Medusa's Bad-Hair Days', by permission of the author; **Judith Nicholls**, 'Mum Says . . .', by permission of the author; **Grace Nichols**, 'My Cousin Melda', by permission of the author; **Trevor Parsons**, 'All About Poets', by permission of the author; **Joan Poulson**, 'Crick Crack Crocodile', by permission of the author; **Julia Rawlinson**, 'A Wonderful Week', by permission of the author; **John Rice**, 'Lost Proprty Ofice', by permission of the author; **Rachel Rooney**, 'Nought to Nine' and 'Unfair', by permission of the author; **Michael Rosen**, 'Words in Space', by permission of the author; **Robert Scotellaro**, 'A Sight for Sore Eyes', by permission of the author; **Fred Sedgwick**, 'Victoria's Poem', by permission of the author; **Andrea Shavick**, 'The Triangular Cruise', by permission of the author; **Nick Toczek**, 'There's a Lot I've Not Seen', by permission of the author; **Jill Townsend**, 'Little Lee', by permission of the author; **Philip Waddell**, 'No Longer My Hero' and 'Bedtime Mysteries', by permission of the author; **Celia Warren**, 'Neversaurus', first published in *Penny Whistle Pete*, ed. David Orme, Collins Educational 1995, and 'Choosing a Book', both by permission of the author; **Colin West**, 'Rolling Down a Hill', by permission of the author; **Kit Wright**, 'Nothing Else', by permission of the author; **Bernard Young**, 'High Queue' and 'Making a Meal of It', first published in *Brilliant* by Kingston Press 2000, by permission of the author.

A selected list of titles available from Macmillan Children's Books

The prices shown below are correct at the time of going to press. However, Macmillan Publishers reserves the right to show new retail prices on covers, which may differ from those previously advertised.

Laugh Out Loud 978-0-330-45456-8 **£4.99**
Chosen by Fiona Waters

I'd Rather Be a Footballer 978-0-330-45713-2 **£4.99**
Chosen by Paul Cookson

I Had a Little Cat –
Collected Poems for Children 978-0-330-46865-7 **£6.99**
Charles Causley

All Pan Macmillan titles can be ordered from our website, www.panmacmillan.com, or from your local bookshop and are also available by post from:

Bookpost, PO Box 29, Douglas, Isle of Man IM99 1BQ

Credit cards accepted. For details:
Telephone: 01624 677237
Fax: 01624 670923
Email: bookshop@enterprise.net
www.bookpost.co.uk

Free postage and packing in the United Kingdom